THE PARABLE OF
DAISY DODDLEPAWS AND THE
WINDY WOODS TREASURE

In Which the Windy Woods Campers Learn
the Biblical Value of Friendship

By Michael Waite
Illustrated by Sheila Lucas

A friend loves you all the time *proverbs 17:17*

Dear Parents: *Read* Daisy Doddlepaws *aloud with your family. Talk about the story and how friends are the best treasure of all. Discuss Proverbs 17:17 and memorize it together. The verse will serve as a reminder of the Christian value of friendship.*

Be sure to look for these other Camp Windy Woods books and toys!

· Digger's Marvelous Moleberry Patch
· Shelby the Magnificent
· Lady Bug Island

· Bartholomew Beaver and the Stupendous Splash
· Butterflies for Two
· Camp Windy Woods Peel and Play

Long before the morning sun peeked down on Clover Patch Cabin, Daisy Doddlepaws was up and getting ready for the big Treasure Hunt. She couldn't imagine why everyone was still asleep on such an important day. She tried to be quiet, but she was so excited that she kept dropping her tools and bumping into things in the dark.

"Shhh!" hissed Priscilla Prickletoes.

"Oopsie… " whispered Daisy, knocking over her pinecone collection.

She carried all the tools and things outside and piled them into her wagon. She put her brand new treasure chest right up front, where it would be ready to fill with treasures. She'd spent all week in the Craft Hut making it look as piratey as possible, so it would be ready for the big Treasure Hunt. She could hardly wait to show it to Anthony Dormouse. He was her best friend, and they were going to be treasure-hunting partners.

She set off for Tumbleroot Cabin to get him.

Daisy was surprised to find that everyone was still asleep in Tumbleroot Cabin, too. She tip-toed over to Anthony's bunk and gave him a shake. His treasure-digging tools were in a pile at the foot of his bunk, and he was wearing his pirate costume.

"Pssst!" she whispered in his ear.

He didn't seem to hear her, so she shook him a little more.

"Hm? What?" he said, trying to sit up. He let out a cough and rubbed his throat. "I feel kind of snuffly," he said. "And my head is all woozy."

"Oh no!" whispered Daisy. "You can't get sick today, Anthony. It's the big Treasure Hunt."

"Pirates don't get sick," said Anthony, and he sneezed.

"I'd better go get Uncle Beardsley just in case," said Daisy.

7

Uncle Beardsley said Anthony had caught a flu-bug. He was feverish and would have to stay in bed for a few days.

"But he'll miss the Treasure Hunt!" cried Daisy.

Uncle Beardsley nodded sadly. "But if he doesn't stay in bed, he won't get well."

"Pirates don't get flu-bugs," Anthony muttered in a sniffly voice. A moment later he was fast asleep.

Daisy felt gloomy and alone as she pulled her wagon up to the Meadow. The Treasure Hunt wasn't going to be much fun without Anthony. She would have to fill her treasure chest all by herself.

By the time she got to the Meadow, everyone was gathered around a big picnic blanket eating snacks. Daisy picked out some things for Anthony—two cookies, a plum, and a big moleberry tart. She wrapped them up in a napkin and dropped them into her treasure chest.

Just then, Uncle Beardsley stood on top of a stump and blew his whistle.

"Hidey-ho, campers!" he shouted. "Is everybody ready to hunt for treasure?"

Everyone hollered and clapped and hopped up and down.

"Then… let the hunt begin!" cried Uncle Beardsley, and he tossed a stack of treasure maps into the air.

The maps fluttered all over the Meadow, and everyone chased after them, laughing and tumbling and bouncing with excitement. Then each of the treasure hunters snatched up a map and scurried into the forest, whooping and cheering. Daisy hurried along behind with her wagon, trying her best to whoop and cheer too.

She followed her treasure map to the edge of the Meadow, but before she could find any treasures, she spotted a big patch of yellow lilies.

"Oh, I'll bet some flowers would make Anthony feel lots better," she thought to herself. So she picked a handful of the yellowest ones and tucked them inside her treasure chest next to the snacks.

Next, she went up to the Orchard where there were supposed to be treasures hidden among the apple trees. But instead, she decided to pick some apples for Anthony. She put them in her treasure chest along with the snacks and flowers.

Just then, Uncle Beardsley came bobbing up the pathway, humming to himself.

"Hullo there, Daisy!" he said. "Finding lots of treasures?"

"Not yet," said Daisy, "I'm picking things to make Anthony feel better."

Uncle Beardsley looked inside her treasure chest and slapped his knee.

"Well, tug my beard!" he said. "You've got a whole chest full of *Windy Woods* treasures!"

"I do?" said Daisy.

"Absolutely!" said Uncle Beardsley. "Lots better than the silly old toys and things you'd find on the Treasure Hunt. Anthony will be the happiest pirate on Lake Willowbye!"

Daisy gazed down at her treasure chest in wonder, and suddenly, she got a wonderful idea.

"Windy Woods treasures!" she cried. "Oh, Anthony will love it!"

Then she thanked Uncle Beardsley and scampered down the path, with her little wagon bouncing merrily after her.

She raced all the way back to Clover Patch Cabin, where she got right to work on her big surprise.

Daisy sat quietly beside Anthony's bunk and waited for him to wake up. She tried very hard not to make any noise, but every time she moved, marbles and pennies tumbled out of her pockets. At last, Anthony began to stir.

"I missed the Treasure Hunt, didn't I?" he said with a gloomy sigh.

"Oh, not really," said Daisy. She was so excited she could hardly hold still. "Maybe you should look under your pillow."

Anthony felt under his pillow and pulled out a little roll of paper. He sat up and opened it anxiously.

"Wowee!" he cried. "It's a treasure map! There's a treasure hidden right here inside the cabin!"

He would've jumped out of bed that very moment if Daisy hadn't stopped him. She made him lie still and tell her where to look for the treasure.

Anthony studied the map carefully. He made
Daisy crawl over bunks and under mattresses. He made
her look up the chimney and tap on the floor boards and
feel along the walls for secret doors, till it seemed as if she'd
gone through the whole cabin, top to bottom.

"It must be a fake," moaned Anthony. He dropped back onto his pillow with a miserable cough and lay there for a long while frowning up at the ceiling. Suddenly, a funny look came over his face, and Daisy laughed because she knew why.

"Look!" he cried, pointing straight above his nose. "There's a great big X under the shelf!" And he jumped out of his sheets, shouting, "X marks the spot! X marks the spot!"

Daisy laughed and clapped and danced around the cabin while Anthony pulled down the treasure from the cupboard.

"It's your pirate chest, Daisy!" he cried. "The one you made for the Treasure Hunt."

"Open it up," said Daisy. "It's for you."

Inside were all the flowers and apples and the snacks she'd gotten from the picnic blanket, along with all sorts of things she'd collected from the forest. There were shiny-smooth stones, and shimmery feathers, and a pinecone shaped just like Priscilla Prickletoes.

"They're Windy Woods treasures," said Daisy. "Uncle Beardsley said they're better than silly old toys."

She helped him back into bed with his chest full of goodies, and tucked the blankets up around his chin.

"Pirates don't usually have best friends," said Anthony. "But I do."

Just then, Barnaby Hopthistle came tumbling through the door. Blossom Sweetpaws rolled in behind him. They both toppled onto the foot of Anthony's bed.

"Howdy-doo!" said Barnaby. "Feeling any better, Anthony?"

"We've got a surprise for you!" said Blossom. She went to the window and pulled open the curtains—and what do you think they saw?

Right outside the cabin window stood Uncle Beardsley and all the campers. They were gathered round a big, crackly campfire which they'd built in just the right spot so Anthony could watch from his bunk. They all waved and shouted "Surprise!" Then everyone burst out singing a loud, happy, hope-you-feel-better-soon sort of camp song.

"Treasures and stuff are okay," Daisy whispered to Anthony. "But friends are best of all."

POTS 'N PANS PARADE

A Friendship March
by Lucy Goosefeathers

Oh, we're marching, marching, we've got our own parade!
Marching, marching, see the friends we've made!
How ever did we come to be
Such a happy company?
We get along so wonderfully!
The Pots 'n Pans Parade!

Oh, we're marching, marching, hand in hand we go.
Marching, marching, isn't it a show!
Anyone can join the fun,
'Cause our parade's for everyone,
Clang-a-banging in the sun!
The Pots 'n Pans Parade!

Chariot Books™ is an imprint of Chariot Family Publishing
Cook Communications, Colorado Springs, CO 80918
Cook Communications, Paris, Ontario
Kingsway Communications, Eastbourne, England

DAISY DODDLEPAWS AND THE WINDY WOODS TREASURE
© 1996 by Michael Waite for text and Sheila Lucas for illustrations